For Ivan
Alice

For Nico
Csil

ALICE BRIÈRE-HAQUET & CSIL

MADAME eiffel

THE LOVE STORY OF THE EIFFEL TOWER

TRANSLATED BY NOELIA HOBEIKA

LITTLE
GESTALTEN

Eiffel is a happy engineer:
young, successful, and in love.

The prettiest girl in Paris is his wife.
Her name is Cathy, and she has a thirst for life.

The earth, the sky, the sea,
there isn't anywhere she doesn't want to be!

For her he builds bridges, train stations,
and theaters so grand.

By sea or by land,
hand in hand,
they travel the globe
and are never apart.

Growing fonder and always going yonder,
until one morning, ...

...a dreary morning,
when Cathy wants to stay in bed.

Eiffel waits a day, then two,
but Cathy still feels blue.

This is so unlike her!
Could Cathy be ill?

No time to waste,
he calls the best doctors in haste.

The most famous, the brightest,
the most reliable, the mightiest,
all come to her bedside and voice their opinions.

Raising their arms in despair,
they agree there is nothing to be done...

Just...perhaps...get some fresh air?

Yes, but how? Traveling is out of the question!
Cathy is much too weak to go on an expedition.

What to do...? What to do...?
Cathy tries to laugh and tells Eiffel with a wink,
"You could build us a railway that takes us up to the clouds in a blink."

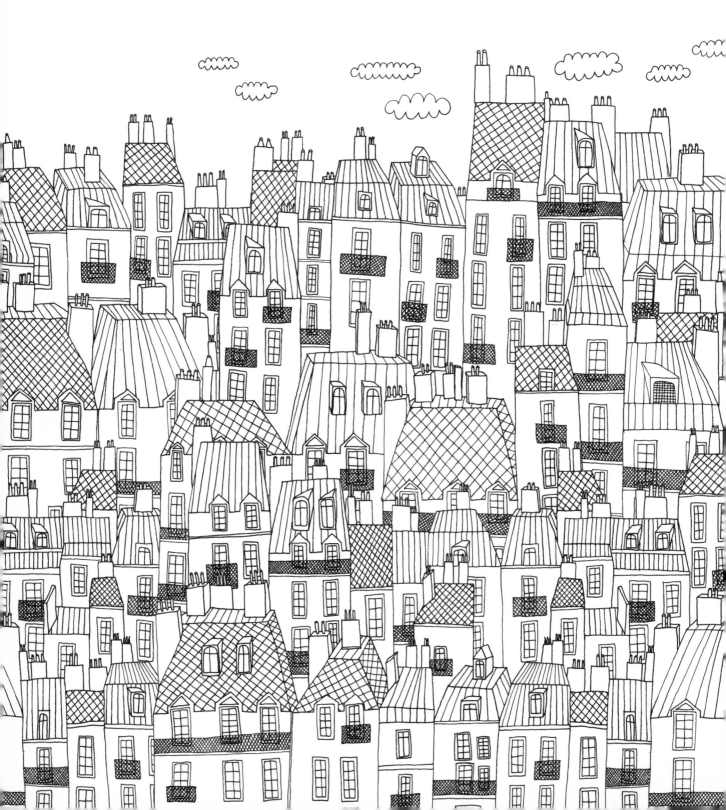

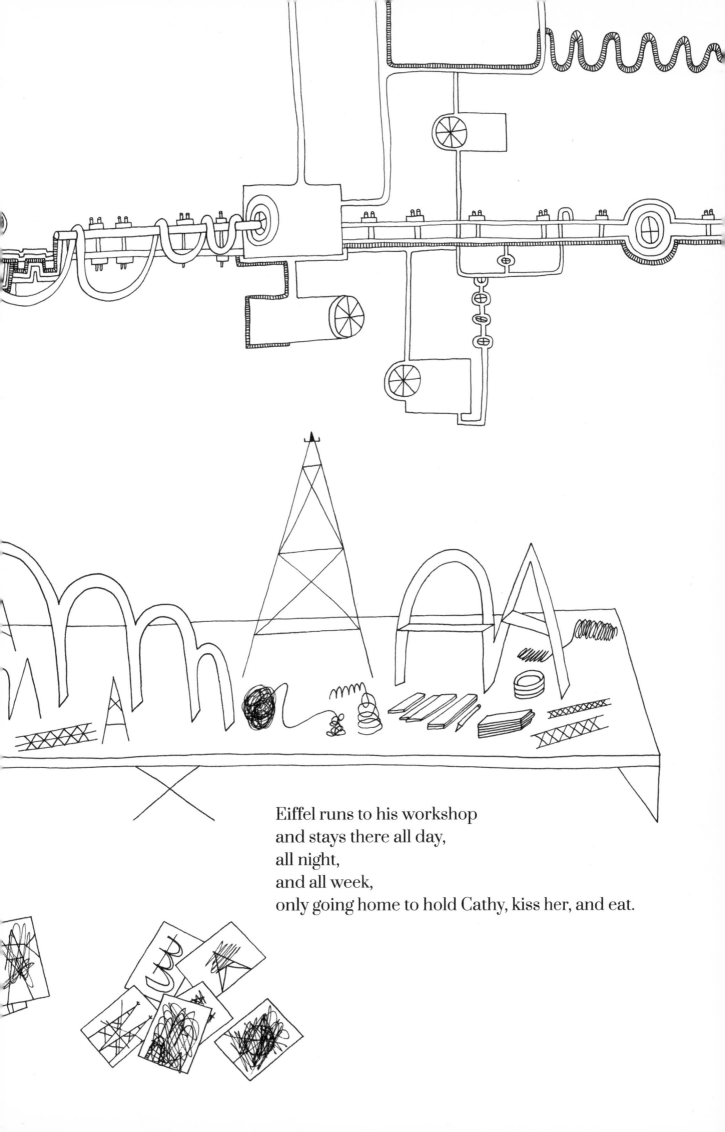

Eiffel runs to his workshop
and stays there all day,
all night,
and all week,
only going home to hold Cathy, kiss her, and eat.

Oh let her fight a bit longer!
She must make it through, she must grow stronger.

But Cathy grows skinny and pale,
and one day she feels it's the end of her tale:

Soon there will be nothing left of the wonderful life
that brought her such joy, such peace, and so little strife.

But when Eiffel returns,
he laughs hysterically. Has he gone crazy?

He takes Cathy in his arms
and dashes through
the streets of the city.

Surprise: there, on the Champs de Mars,

an immense tower rises up to the clouds!

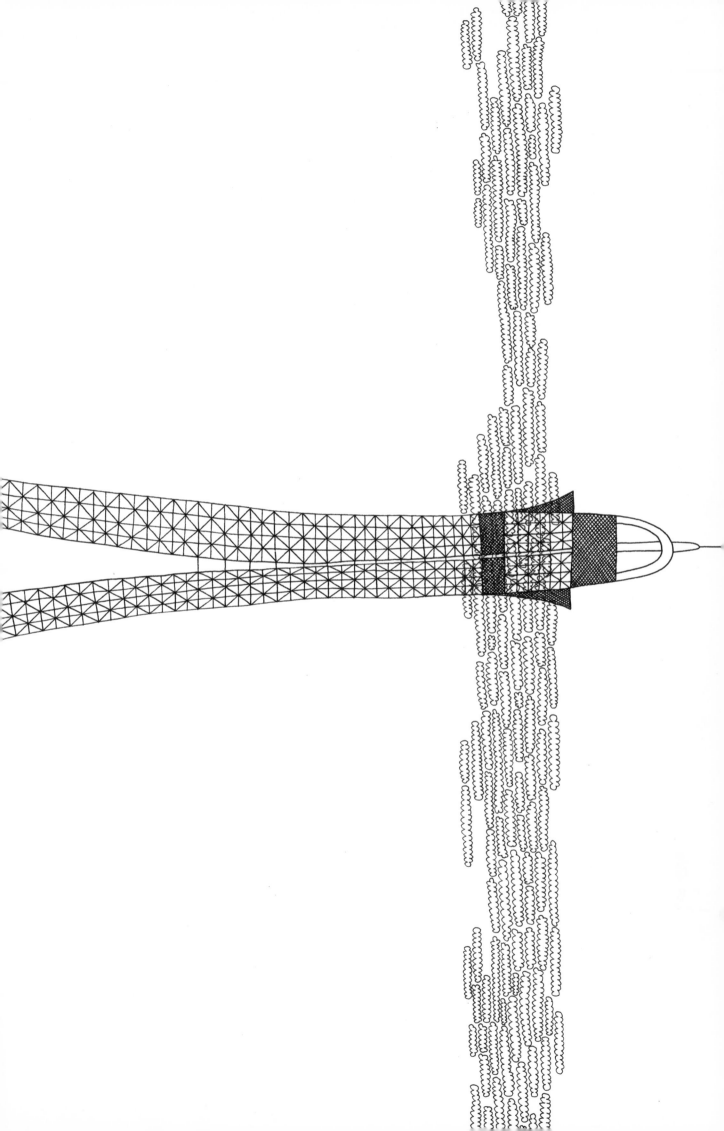

With Cathy still in his arms,
Eiffel climbs up the tower.

First floor...
                Second floor...

No, it's not too late!

Third floor...
...a miracle awaits!

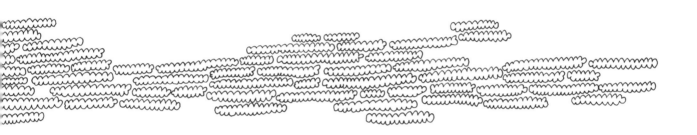

Cathy's cheeks turn rosy,
her eyes sparkle again.

Watching the river Seine,
the children on the carousels,
and, above the roofs,
the sunrise reflecting in each other's eyes,
Cathy and Eiffel lived happily and well for a long time.

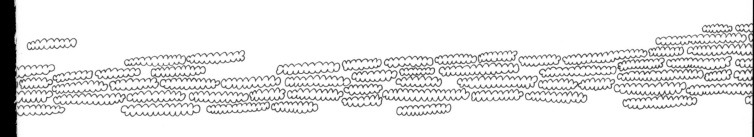

Who knows, maybe they are still there?

Rumor has it that sometimes at night
you can see their shadow appear in the street light.

Madame Eiffel
The Love Story of the Eiffel Tower

by Alice Brière-Haquet (Text)
and Csil (Illustrations)

Translated from the French by Noelia Hobeika
Published by Little Gestalten, Berlin 2015
ISBN: 978-3-89955-755-8

Typeface: Prata by Cyreal
Printed by Eberl Print GmbH, Immenstadt im Allgäu
Made in Germany

THE FRENCH ORIGINAL EDITION MME EIFFEL WAS PUBLISHED BY ÉDITIONS
FRIMOUSSE © FOR THE FRENCH ORIGINAL: ÉDITIONS FRIMOUSSE, 2015 © FOR THE
ENGLISH EDITION: LITTLE GESTALTEN, AN IMPRINT OF DIE GESTALTEN VERLAG GMBH
& CO. KG, BERLIN 2015. TRANSLATION RIGHTS ARRANGED THROUGH THE VEROK
AGENCY, BARCELONA, SPAIN.

FOR MORE INFORMATION, PLEASE VISIT LITTLE.GESTALTEN.COM.

BIBLIOGRAPHIC INFORMATION PUBLISHED BY THE DEUTSCHE NATIONALBIBLIOTHEK:
THE DEUTSCHE NATIONALBIBLIOTHEK LISTS THIS PUBLICATION IN THE DEUTSCHE
NATIONALBIBLIOGRAFIE; DETAILED BIBLIOGRAPHIC DATA ARE AVAILABLE ONLINE AT
HTTP://DNB.D-NB.DE.

THIS BOOK WAS PRINTED ON PAPER CERTIFIED ACCORDING TO THE
STANDARDS OF THE FSC®.